A Surprise for Gappy

A Surprise for Gappy

Book One of
The Young Vampire Adventures
by
Star Donovan

Illustrations and cover art
by
Ann-Cathrine Loo

Bronwynn Press

Gappy and Bronwynn Press are trademarks of
Bronwynn Press, LLC.

Published by
Bronwynn Press, LLC
PO Box 297
Troy, New York 12182

First Edition, 2008
Library of Congress Control Number: 2008938506
ISBN-13: 978-0-9821404-0-6
ISBN-10: 0-9821404-0-1

Bronwynn Press

Contents

Chapter One

A Face Full of Paint

A part from merrily driving his parents mad with his favorite habit of whistling between his top front teeth, nine-year-old Gappy was really a very nice boy, despite having a really dumb name. In a moment of silliness, Cuthbert and Livinia Grapple had named their baby son Gustavus and, well, who could live with a name like *that!*

When he first started kindergarten at

Catchpole Elementary School, Gappy's class-mates had quickly nicknamed him Crappy Gappy, or Crabapple for short. When he reached the second grade, lost his top front teeth and discovered he could whistle through the gap, they shortened his name again to just Gappy. Though not very flattering, it was still a big improvement on Gustavus Grapple.

Gappy was tall and skinny with very pale skin and longish, black hair that was forever flopping down over his forehead and into his blue eyes. His best friend was a short, red-haired girl named Pru, who lived a few blocks down the street from Gappy's house. Her face and arms were covered with ginger-colored freckles, and the other kids called her Carrots because of her flaming red hair and eyebrows.

One of the reasons he and Pru got along

so well, thought Gappy, trotting up the steps to school and trying to blow a humongous bubble with his watermelon bubble gum, was because she also had the misfortune of having a really dumb name — Prudence Pottage.

That afternoon, Gappy fainted in art class. When his head hit his desk, he smeared blue and yellow paint all over the side of his face and in his hair. The next thing he knew, his teacher, Miss Pinsweep, was wiping his face with a tissue while Pru fanned air at him with a book, her freckled face screwed up in concentration and concern for her friend.

Gappy sat up and looked around. His classmates were all staring at him, some with their mouths hanging open in a most unattractive manner.

"What?" he asked. "Why's everyone looking at me? What happened?"

"Well, dear, I think you fainted," Miss Pinsweep told him. "The principal is calling your mother now, and I expect she'll come and take you home."

"Hey, Gappy, you got paint on your face," yelled smart-mouth Billy Tompkins from the third row. "It's dripping all over the place!"

Some of the kids snickered.

"That's enough, William," snapped Miss Pinsweep.

She took a second tissue from her desk, dipped it in some clean water and wiped Gappy's face again.

"There, that's better. I can't do much about the yellow streaks in your hair, but it doesn't look too bad. You can pretend they're highlights. Now, how do you feel?"

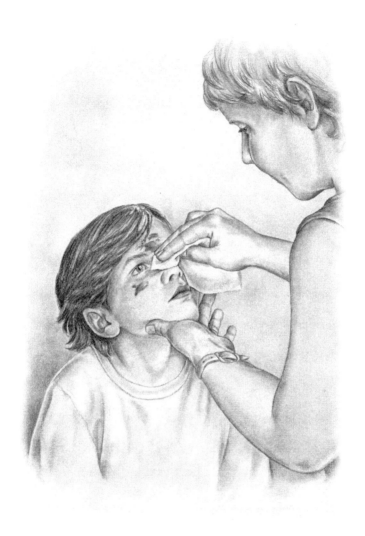

She took a second tissue from her desk, dipped it in some
clean water and wiped Gappy's face again.

Gappy thought for a moment. "Well, I do feel a bit dizzy, Miss Pinsweep, but most of all I'm really, really hungry. Do you think I could have something to eat?"

"Here, Miss Pinsweep, I have some cookies," called Rebecca Jones from the back of the class. She jumped up, her mousy-colored braids swinging wildly as she enthusiastically waved a paper bag in the air. It had a hole in the bottom, and crumbs sprayed out all over her desk.

"Thank you, Rebecca," said Miss Pinsweep, smiling at her eagerness. "Please bring them here, and then you can clear up those crumbs."

Gappy munched the two chocolate-chip cookies he found in the bag, but the hungry feeling did not go away. His stomach felt like it was flopping about like a fish out of water and at one point gave such a loud rumble that everyone heard. It was very embarrassing.

"Goodness, Gustavus!" exclaimed Miss Pinsweep. "I guess you *must* be hungry. Well, your mother should be here soon, and you can ask her to give you some more lunch."

Soon Gappy's mom arrived and stood just inside the classroom door, fiddling with the belt on her smart, gray skirt and looking around for the teacher.

"Ah, Mrs. Grapple, there you are," Miss Pinsweep called to her. "Gappy seems okay now, just a little dizzy, but he says he's very hungry, even though we just ate lunch. He just finished up Rebecca's cookies too."

"Thanks, Miss Pinsweep," Livinia Grapple said. She smiled and held out her hand.

"Come on, Gappy. Let's take you home, shall we?"

Gappy stood up carefully. He did feel quite wobbly and empty and was glad he could go home. Pru put his homework in his book bag for him and gave it to Mrs. Grapple, and then Gappy and his mom walked down the corridor and out the big front doors of the school.

Chapter Two

A Trip to the Emergency Room

After Gappy was settled in the back seat of the car with his seat belt fastened, his mother turned to look over her shoulder at him. "Now, Gappy," she said, "I don't want you to worry, but I'm taking you to the hospital for some tests. I know you've never been sick enough to go to the hospital, but there's really nothing to be afraid of. The doctors are very nice and won't hurt you. We just need to find out why you fainted, okay?"

"Will they give me a shot?" Gappy asked. He did not like getting shots.

"I don't think so," Mom said, "but they might need to take some blood from your arm to test it. If they do, it'll just be a little prick and I'll be right there, okay?"

"O—kay." Gappy looked doubtful. Taking blood sounded like getting a shot that went on for a long time.

Mom laughed at his expression. "It'll be over very quickly, I promise," she said.

When they reached the hospital, Mom parked the car and they walked up the marble steps and through the heavy glass doors into the emergency room.

A plump woman was sitting behind the reception desk. She smiled at Gappy. "Hello, young sir, and what's the matter with you?"

"I fainted in class," Gappy answered. She seemed a nice woman — sort of jolly and cuddly all over, her hair in a curly, blond Afro.

"Oh dear," the woman said, "and what's your name?"

"This is Gustavus Grapple and I'm his mother," Mrs. Grapple told her.

The woman asked them some questions, and Mom filled out some paperwork. Then a tall nurse took them into a side room, asked them some more questions and took Gappy's blood pressure and pulse.

"The doctor will be out in a minute if you'd like to go back and sit down," she said when she was finished.

Gappy and his mother sat down in the waiting room, and Gappy tried reading some of the books in the bookcase – not that he felt much like reading. He kept thinking about the long-lasting shot. He just wished they would call his name and get it over with.

After a while, a young doctor came out to the waiting room. He was wearing blue jeans and a short, white coat with a big smiley-face name tag that had the words "Dr. Smitty" printed on it in day-glo yellow letters. Gappy supposed the man had to wear the white coat so people would know he was a doctor. Otherwise, he looked just like one of his friends' dads.

"Hello," said Doctor Smitty, smiling at Gappy and his mother. "Are you the fella who fainted at school today?"

Gappy nodded.

"Right then, if you'll come with me, please?"

The doctor led them into an examination room where a long, white bed stood against the wall. "Now, sit up here, Gustavus," he said. "That's it. I'm going to listen to your breathing and your heart, okay?"

Gappy got up onto the high, narrow bed. The doctor washed his hands and then listened to Gappy's chest with his stethoscope. He looked in Gappy's eyes and ears and made him say "Ah" so he could look down his throat. Then he tapped Gappy's knees, making them jerk up and down all by themselves.

"Well, I would say you're a healthy young man," Doctor Smitty announced, washing his hands again. "Now, I have to take a little blood from you, just in case, so I don't miss anything, all right? Then we'll be all set. Can you roll up your sleeve for me?"

Gappy rolled up his sleeve and looked the other way while Dr. Smitty took some blood from the inside of his elbow. It was not too bad after all. Then he had to wait outside in the waiting room while his mom talked to the doctor.

She came out in a few minutes, and they walked out to the car.

"Can I have something to eat now?" Gappy asked when they got home.

"Sure, Gappy," Mom said. "Why don't you go upstairs and lie down, and I'll bring you a peanut butter and jelly sandwich. Then you can have a nap until Dad gets home."

Gappy climbed the stairs to his bedroom. He did feel quite tired, and his legs felt like lead. It would be nice to take a nap after eating his sandwich.

Chapter Three

Startling News

When Cuthbert Grapple came home that evening, Mom called Gappy to come downstairs. His parents were sitting in the living room, and he went in and sat next to Dad on the couch. Mom was eyeing him with a funny look that made him feel somewhat uncomfortable, and Gappy could sense some tension in the room as if his parents had been arguing.

He turned to look at his father. "Hey, Dad, did you hear what happened today at school?"

"I sure did," Dad said, giving his son a quick hug. His mustache felt scratchy against Gappy's cheek. "It must have been pretty scary, huh? Now, I want you to listen carefully, Gappy, because Mom and I have to talk to you about something very important."

"Humph," said Mom. She stood up, shook her head at Dad and began pacing as if she were worried about something.

Gappy looked at her. "I'm not sick, am I? The doctor said I was fine."

"No, you're not sick, Gappy," she said, "but —"

"— but you know how you were feeling so hungry and dizzy?" Dad interrupted. "Well, that's what we have to talk to you about."

Gappy sat up straight. This sounded like serious stuff and a bit scary.

Dad coughed and cleared his throat.

Mom stopped pacing for a moment and put her hands on her hips. "Burt," she said, "do you really think we ought to do this now? I mean, what if it's a false alarm? Maybe we should wait and see."

"No, Liv," Dad said. "We should tell him now. I think it's time. I think it's starting to happen."

This all sounded very mysterious to Gappy. "What, Dad?" he asked. "What's starting to happen?"

Dad shifted on the couch to get more comfortable. "Well, let's see. How should I say this? Okay. Well . . . hmm . . . er . . ."

Gappy bounced on the couch with impatience, jiggling Dad up and down. "Come on, Dad, spit it out. I can take it."

"I hope so," Mom murmured very softly to herself.

Dad frowned at her, then took a deep breath and cleared his throat once more. "Okay, here goes, Gappy . . . er . . . have you ever heard of vampires?"

This was so different from what Gappy was expecting Dad to say that he just gawked at his parents.

They looked back at him, expectantly.

After a few minutes of staring at one another, Gappy realized his dad actually did want an answer to his odd question, so he said, "Yeah, sure, Dad. Vampires are bad people in stories, who suck people's blood to stay alive."

After a few minutes of staring at one another, Gappy realized
his dad actually did want an answer to his odd question.

"Well, maybe in the olden days they were bad," said Dad, "but this is the twenty-first century and vampires have come a long way since then. They're not all bad, nowadays."

"Oh, Dad —" Gappy interrupted, but his father held up his hand for him to keep quiet.

"I know most people think they are just scary stories," he continued, "but there *really are* vampires."

"No there aren't," Gappy laughed. "That's silly, Dad. They're just stories. Mom, tell Dad he's talking crazy."

He looked at their serious faces and stamped his foot in frustration. "And why are we talking about vampires anyway? What's that got to do with anything?"

Mom pushed back a long strand of silky, black hair behind her ear. "This is very important, Gappy," she said. "Dad's not joking."

"Right," Dad said. "I know it sounds crazy and can't possibly be true, but there really *are* vampires. And, what's more, Mom and I are vampires and it looks like you are too."

Chapter Four

Crazy Parents!

Gappy sat with his mouth open, looking from Mom to Dad and waiting for them to smile and say it was all a joke, but they did not. In fact, they were not smiling at all. They looked very serious, especially Mom, who seemed as if she were really angry with Dad.

His mother sighed. "We did hope you weren't going to turn into a vampire like your dad and I. You see, often the children of vampires stay normal humans and never become vampires themselves. If it *is* going to happen, their bodies usually begin changing around the time of their ninth birthday. Well, you're nine years old now, Gappy, and we think you're becoming one. That's why you fainted today and felt dizzy and hungry. I wanted to wait until you were a little older, but Dad thought we should tell you now because the hungry-dizzy spells are probably going to start happening more and more often."

"No!" Gappy shouted, his eyes bugging out in confusion and fright. He felt as if he were in the *Twilight Zone.* He jumped up from the couch and punched his fists against his thighs.

"This is stupid! You're both crazy!" he

yelled. "Vampires aren't real. You're making it up. Why're you trying to frighten me?"

"Listen to me," Dad commanded, leaning forward on the couch to look his son straight in the eye. "It's true. I know it's really scary and difficult for you to believe, but you'll have to face it. You *are* a vampire. The blood test at the hospital proves that you're anemic. That means you need more iron in your blood for your body to make red blood cells. All humans need iron, but vampires need more of it than regs . . . er . . . regular humans do."

"You . . . you mean you . . . we . . . uh . . . vampires aren't human?" Gappy stammered.

Mom snorted.

"Of course we're human," Dad said, chuckling. "We're just like regular humans — vampires call them regs for short — but with a little extra special something about us, that's all. Actually, a *lot* of extra special somethings."

"But, Dad! Vampires bite people's necks to suck their blood!" Gappy gulped in a strangled voice as his throat suddenly closed with fear. He wrinkled his nose in disgust and rubbed it hard. "That's gross! I could *never* do that!"

"Oh, Gappy, you don't have to bite people's necks, like you see in the movies," said Mom, gently. "As Dad told you, we're *modern* vampires. It's true that our ancestors used to suck blood in the olden days, but what vampires do now is eat lots of liver and kidneys, raw red meat and other foods that contain a lot of iron. Plus, they take vitamins and iron supplements so they don't have to bite people's necks to survive. And no one ever has to know that they — we — are vampires."

"Liver and kidneys and raw meat? That's yuck and double gross!" Gappy looked to his father for reassurance. "Is that true, Dad?"

Dad nodded, smiling at his son's horrified expression. "Yes, it is. It might seem gross to you now, but you'll get used to it. As I said, it's really a lot simpler being a vampire these days."

"So, we're not like Dracula then?" Gappy asked in a small voice.

"No," Dad chuckled. "We're not like Dracula."

Gappy thought for a moment. "But what are people going to say? The kids will tease me so much at school. No one will want to be my friend. They'll all be scared of me."

"Gappy," Mom said, kneeling down by

Dad. She reached out with her long, white fingers and took both of Gappy's hands in hers. "You can never, ever, *ever* tell anyone. It has to be a secret. It's *our* secret, just us, the Grapple family, okay?"

"I can't even tell Pru?" Gappy asked.

Dad shook his head. "No, Gappy. Not even Pru."

Mom shook her head too. "People just wouldn't understand if you told them. For one thing, they wouldn't believe you and, yes, it would give them a big excuse for teasing you.

"And what would happen if they *did* believe you? Would you like to have scientists poking and prodding you and keeping you locked up like an animal so they could study you? They'd want to write papers about you and talk about you on TV, in newspapers and magazines, like you were something strange, scary and dangerous. Would that be fun?"

"No—o—o," Gappy said, shaking his head and rubbing his nose again.

A thought struck him. "Hey, Dad? What about sleeping in coffins in the daytime, and stuff like that? How come you don't do that either?"

Dad laughed, his mustache crinkling as he grinned. "Well, over the years vampires have gotten more used to the sunshine. As long as we're careful every day about using special sunscreen that some of our vampire scientists have invented, the sun doesn't bother us too badly."

Gappy shook his head. This was all a bit much to take in and understand all at once.

He looked solemnly at his parents and they looked back at him, Mom still kneeling by his dad. Thoughts were churning around in his head. He wanted to know so many things, but he felt so hyper suddenly that he could not think of the questions to ask.

Everyone was silent for a few moments, lost in their own worlds.

"Well, I think I'd better go and fix dinner," Mom said after a while, getting up and heading for the kitchen.

She stopped in the doorway and looked back at Gappy, who was still standing in the middle of the room, whistling softly between his teeth and trying to get his thoughts together. "I know this has been a big shock for you, Gappy. It's a lot to take in and think about, and you'll probably need a day or two to get used to the idea. Why don't you go get your homework and come and keep me company in the kitchen?"

Dad patted his son on the shoulder and picked up his newspaper. "That's a good idea, Livvie."

Gappy went upstairs to his room. *Boy, do I feel weird!* he thought. *Sort of wobbly and excited inside, like I'm starting out on a big adventure that might be fun but difficult too. I wonder if that's how my friend Lucy felt when her parents told her she was adopted. Like she was suddenly a different person than she'd always thought she was.*

Yeah, that's it, Gappy nodded to himself. *I used to be a normal kid, but now I'm suddenly something different. I mean, I'm still me but I'm not the same me. Am I a better me, or a worse me, and what's going to happen next?*

He shook his head. *I should do what Miss Pinsweep tells us in class when people are getting hyper. Think of one thing at a time, then move on to the next thing. Yeah, that's what I'll do. I just can't think straight like this. There are so many things going around in my head, I feel like I'm going to explode!*

Chapter Five

Meatloaf and Superman

Gappy rummaged in his book bag and took out his school books. Then he went back downstairs and sat at the kitchen table while Mom bustled about making one of his favorite dishes — meatloaf. As the warm smells of hamburger, ketchup and spices filled the kitchen, Gappy started his homework. He did not have much to do because he had only been at school half a day.

He soon finished his sums and worked on a couple of paragraphs for English class about his favorite pet. Since he did not own a pet, he wrote about a rabbit that he had once rescued and kept in a box until its injured leg was better. Then he chewed on his pencil and watched his mother, who was now making some Jell-O for dessert.

"So, Mom," he said. "What's it like being a vampire? Am I going to be very different now?"

"Well," Mom answered, ruffling his hair, "there's no rush. The change doesn't happen overnight but gradually over time. I don't think it's a good idea to overload that brain of yours right now with too much information. After all, you've just had a big shock. You'll find out all there is to know soon enough."

"But, Mom!" Gappy protested. "You can't just tell me one minute I'm turning into a vampire and then not tell me anything else."

Mom pursed her lips and looked stubborn. "In time, Gappy. In time."

Gappy turned to Dad, who had come into the kitchen just then. "Dad," he complained, "I want to know more, but Mom won't tell me."

Dad sniffed. "Is dinner ready?" he asked. "It sure smells good." He eyed Gappy. "Even though it *is* cooked," he added.

"Okay, that's gross, Dad!" Gappy cried. "And don't change the subject."

Dad looked at Mom. "Livinia?"

"Burt?" Mom said.

"Don't you think we could tell Gappy just a little more?" Dad asked.

Mom sighed. "I don't think he's ready, Burt. He's only nine years old and his world's just been turned upside down. This is a life-changing event for him. Give it time, that's what *I* think."

"But, Dad," Gappy persisted, sensing he would have an easier time getting Dad to agree he needed to know more. "Can't you just tell me one thing vampires can do that humans . . . er . . . regs can't do? Then I'll be quiet, I promise."

Dad looked at Mom. "I don't think it'll hurt to tell him one small thing, Liv." He made a funny face at her.

Mom laughed. She never could keep a straight face when Dad started acting silly.

"How about telepathy?" Dad suggested.

Mom sighed. "Go on, then. I guess that's a

good one to start with, seeing as it's one of the talents that comes first."

"What's telepathy?" Gappy asked, excited that he was going to learn more.

"It's like mind reading," Dad answered.

"Wow!" Gappy marveled. "Like knowing what people are thinking? That sounds neat. Maybe this vampire business won't be too bad after all. When will *I* be able to do that?"

Mom started laying the table for dinner, slapping the plates down harder than she needed to as if to show her disapproval.

"Well," Dad said, "you'll probably notice one day that someone says something you were just thinking about. It happens to every-one at some time or another, but when it starts happening more often, you'll know it's your talent getting stronger."

Mom sighed again as she took the meatloaf out of the oven. "You must be very careful, though, Gappy. Vampires have to take an oath that they won't use their talents, except for the good of mankind or in emergency situations. It's called the Vampire Code of Conduct. It's not all fun and games, you know. It's a big responsibility."

"She's right," Dad agreed. "Hmm. Let me think of an example. You remember the Superman movie, don't you?"

Gappy nodded.

"Well, I'm not saying we can do what Superman does, but you can see what a big responsibility it was for Superman to both hide and use his talents."

"Cool! So are you saying we're a *bit* like Superman?" Gappy asked.

But Dad had his head stuck in the fridge looking for some mustard, and Mom was taking napkins out of a drawer and would say no more except, "Dinner's ready."

Chapter Six

A Secret Identity

Early the next morning, Gappy dreamed that his right hand was tingling. When he woke up, the sun was shining in at the window sending a bright beam of golden light across his bed and his hand. Suddenly, everything he had learned the night before flooded into his head, and his heart almost stopped with excitement. He snatched his hand out of the sunlight and inspected it closely. It looked a little pinker than his other hand, but it had stopped tingling now the sun was no longer shining on it.

He lay back on his pillow and stared up at the ceiling, thinking about what his parents had told him the night before.

"I'm a vampire," he whispered to himself after a while.

"I'm a vampire!" he said a little louder.

An excited feeling started to well up in his chest until he could hold it in no longer.

"I'M A VAMPIRE!" he yelled at the top of his voice.

Mom popped her head around the door. "Are you all right, Gappy?"

Gappy nodded. "Yeah, Mom. I was just thinking about everything and I had to let it out."

He snatched his hand out of the sunlight
and inspected it closely.

"Well, so long as it's in the house where no one else can hear," Mom said, "but nowhere else, mind? Do you feel well enough to go to school?"

Gappy scrambled out of bed. "Yeah, I can't *wait* to go to school!"

Mom shot him a warning glance.

"Okay, Mom, I know. I won't tell anyone. I just feel full of energy today, that's all."

"Well, that's good, I guess," Mom said. "Breakfast in ten minutes?"

Gappy hummed as he got dressed and loaded his book bag. "This is the first day of the rest of my life," he hummed. *Isn't that a song on one of the oldies radio stations? Well, that's what I feel like.* A lovely smell wafted upstairs and Gappy sniffed in approval. *Mmm, bacon.*

He pounded down the stairs, almost colliding with Dad, who was coming out of the bathroom.

"Watch it, young scamp!" Dad gasped. "And watch it down those stairs!" he yelled as Gappy went tearing past. "You can't fly yet, you know."

But Gappy did not hear. He was too busy concentrating on the bacon smell.

As he sat eating his breakfast, Mom handed him some pills with his glass of orange juice. "Here, Gappy, you have to start taking these now," she said, sitting down next to him with her teacup. "The big red one's your iron pill and the others are vitamins that help keep vampires healthy. They're made for us 'specially by Benny's V.I.P. in San Francisco."

"V.I.P.? As in Very Important Person?"

Gappy asked. He gulped down the pills with a swig of orange juice. "That wasn't so bad but the purple one tastes like poop. Yuck!"

Mom laughed. "Well, get used to it. We've been complaining for years, but Mr. Benny just can't seem to make it taste any better. And V.I.P. stands for Vampire Invigorational Pharmacy." She smiled as Gappy sounded out the long title. "It *is* rather a mouthful, isn't it? That's why vampires call it V.I.P. for short. The regs probably think it stands for Very Important Pharmacy, which may seem a little puzzling because to them it just looks like a regular drugstore. Mr. Benny's very careful to keep the vampire potions hidden away under lock and key."

She took a sip of her tea. "Oh, and I might as well warn you my cooking's going to be getting a bit different from now on too."

Gappy wrinkled his nose, remembering the mention last night of raw meat, liver and kidneys, and stuff like that. Did that mean no more meatloaf, or would it be *raw* meatloaf from now on?

The school day dragged for Gappy. He felt so different. Everything seemed brighter and louder and, well, clearer somehow. Except for Billy Tompkins nudging him in the ribs as he ran past and hissing, "Gonna faint today, Gappy?" nobody took any more notice of him than usual. He could not believe that no one could tell he was different – not even Pru, though she did say at one point that he seemed to be having trouble concentrating. He felt as if there were loads of fizzy soda bubbles filling up his chest, dying to burst out, and he felt very conscious of the heavy secret he had to hide from everyone.

My secret identity, Gappy thought to himself. *Oh, it's so hard having something you're excited about but can't tell anyone!* Several times, he almost blurted out something to Pru, but then the image of white-coated scientists poking at him came into his head, and he closed his mouth just in time. He hugged himself hard and shook his head violently as if to get rid of some of the excitement fizzing up into his brain.

I suppose it'll get easier once I've grown used to it, he tried to tell himself, *but —*

"Everything okay, Gappy?" Miss Pinsweep called.

"Yes, Miss Pinsweep," Gappy answered and bent over his book with a little smile.

Chapter Seven

Gappy to the Rescue

After school, Gappy walked home with Pru as usual. Almost at the corner of her street grew a hedge that straggled along the front of an old, abandoned house. As they approached the hedge, they could hear a boy's jeering laughter and a dog barking. It sounded like the fourth-grade bully, Billy Tompkins, and his dog Butch — an enormous Rottweiler, who was just as mean as his master.

Gappy and Pru looked at each other and stopped walking when they heard another boy's voice pleading, "Don't do it, Billy. Please. I worked so hard on that, and my dad's going to be really mad if it gets broken. He spent a long time helping me glue it together."

They peered through a hole in the hedge and saw Billy Tompkins standing on the right side of the empty house's wraparound porch, holding a model of a big, white building above his head. He was obviously threatening to throw it over the railing onto the stone path that wound around the house.

Butch sat on the porch at the top of a short flight of steps, growling at Timothy Daylo. The boy was standing on the front path, halfway to the house, but too scared of the dog to approach any farther.

"Gosh, that's Timmy's model of the White House," Gappy whispered to Pru. Timmy had brought it to school for Citizen's Day, and the principal had placed it in a glass display case in the entrance hall for a whole week for people to see and admire.

"You're right," Pru whispered back. "He told everyone how it took him and his dad simply ages to make it. His dad's been laid off from his job so he's home a lot more. He and Timmy worked on it together."

"Yeah, he's so proud of that model," Gappy said, "and now Billy's going to break it. Poor Timmy."

Timothy Daylo was a short, thin boy with wispy hair that refused to lie flat. He had a lazy eye, so he wore thick spectacles that made one eye look huge, while the other lens of his glasses was covered by a piece of bright pink tape. He was just asking to be bullied by people like Billy Tompkins, who had quickly nicknamed him Timmy Day-Glo.

"What shall we do?" Pru asked. "We can't just do *nothing*."

Gappy did not answer. He was not particularly scared of Billy, who was a year older from having to repeat fourth grade. Although the boy was fatter than Gappy, he was not much taller and he *was* pretty stupid — not that anyone would ever say that to his face. It was too dangerous.

However, Gappy *was* scared of Butch. He had seen him snap at one or two kids when they got too close to Billy.

He and Pru walked down to a gap in the hedge where a gate had once stood. They could see more clearly now, but what could they do?

"Stay here, Pru," Gappy decided. "I might be able to do something, but you're smaller than me, and a girl, and I'm sure Billy wouldn't mind hitting a girl just as much as a boy."

Pru looked indignant. "I'm just as game as you are, Gustavus Grapple. Even if I *am* a girl."

"Just the same, stay here," Gappy told her. He ran down the front path to join Timmy, who glanced sideways at him with a worried look.

"Billy!" Gappy yelled.

"Yeah, what do *you* want?" Billy yelled

back. "Hey, it's the fainting boy, Crappy Gappy, come to the rescue. And is that your little girlfriend Carrots I see? Aw, ain't that cute. Well, you're too late."

He raised the White House higher above his head and planted his feet, preparing to chuck the model over the railing.

"Don't do it, Billy. Don't be such a bully," Pru shouted from close behind Gappy.

Gappy sighed, but he was only slightly surprised. He might have known Pru would not listen to him when he told her to stay back.

As Timmy wailed a final, "No—o—o," and Butch barked again, Gappy felt a surge of anger sweep through him. Suddenly, the fizzy bubbles in his chest seemed to pop and his mind became crystal clear. Before he knew what he was doing, he had dropped his book bag and was running down the path the rest of the way to the house.

Shut up, stupid dog, he thought to himself as he ran.

No sooner had Gappy finished this thought, than Butch yelped loudly and cowered down on the porch. Billy lowered his arms a little and looked sideways at Butch as Gappy skidded to a halt near the foot of the steps. The dog stared down at Gappy and began whimpering. Timmy, who had crept up to join Gappy, shoved his glasses up his nose with a grubby hand and gaped at Butch, his mouth open in a round O.

Time seemed to stop for a moment and everyone froze except for Butch, who kept on whimpering.

Gappy's thoughts were still as clear as crystal, and he still felt really angry.

But, what just happened?

He looked at Butch. *Yeah, you stupid dog.*

Butch yelped again and snarled at Gappy.

Wow! Gappy wondered. *Can that dog hear my thoughts?*

"Fsssss," he whistled softly to himself between his teeth. He stared intently at Butch and concentrated hard, imagining he could send a beam from his own head to Butch's furry one, aiming right between the ears.

Go away, Butch, he thought slowly and deliberately. *Go home.*

To his amazement, Butch whined loudly and scampered down the steps, then hurtled past the two boys and up the path, almost knocking Pru over in the process.

Butch yelped again and snarled at Gappy.

"Hey!" she yelled, but the dog was gone, racing down the street with his tail between his legs.

"What!" Billy gasped. "Whaddidya do to 'im?"

"Me? Nothing," Gappy said. "What *could* I do to him?"

Billy looked puzzled. His arms had sunk even lower so that the White House was now almost sitting on the top of his head. He felt torn. Should he go check on his dog, or finish what he had set out to do — destroy the model? He looked at Gappy standing at the foot of the steps with Timmy cowering behind him. And to make matters worse, there was that dratted, carroty-haired Pru as well.

As Gappy gazed coolly back at Billy, not seeming in the least bit frightened, Billy suddenly imagined what he must look like to the others — a burly boy with a red face and a round pudding-bowl haircut, like a stupid monk holding a stupid model above his head.

All of a sudden, he felt really ridiculous!

"Argh, whatever!" he shouted and threw the White House over the railing.

Pru and Timmy gasped, but Gappy had guessed what Billy was about to do. He quickly ran to the side and caught the model in his arms, just before it hit the ground.

Billy ran down the steps and up the path, aiming a kick at Timmy as he passed the boy. "Grow some guts, will ya?" he shouted. "Get ya later, Crappy," he yelled over his shoulder as he brushed past Pru. Then he ran off down the street after Butch.

Timmy and Pru came over to Gappy.

"Gappy, you were great!" Timmy squealed.

Pru nodded in agreement. "Yeah. I don't know what you did, but for some reason that dog doesn't like you."

"I don't know why," Gappy said, handing the model to Timmy. "Just lucky, I guess. Anyway, here's your model, Timmy. It's a little bent there where I grabbed it but it looks okay."

"That's all right," Timmy said. "My dad and I will easily fix that. Gee, thanks a lot, Gappy. I owe you one. See you at school tomorrow?"

"Yeah," Gappy said. "See you tomorrow."

"Bye," Pru called after him as Timmy trotted up the path. He was eager to get home to fix his model.

She picked up Gappy's book bag and

handed it to him. Then she slipped her arm into his. "That was weird," she said. "Butch seemed like he was really scared of you all of a sudden. What did you do? Hypnotize him or something?"

Gappy squirmed. "Don't be silly," he told her. "Haven't you heard people say that dogs and horses and things are supposed to know what people are feeling? Maybe Butch could tell that I wasn't going to let him scare me, so he ran away. I'm just glad it happened the way it did. I wasn't looking forward to getting beaten up by Billy, and he still would have smashed Timmy's model."

Pru scratched her head and twisted a red pigtail round and round with her finger before sticking the spiky end in her mouth. "Well, I just know it was really weird the way Butch acted and how you two were looking at each other, like you had some sort of a connection."

Gappy squirmed some more. Little did Pru know, but she had almost guessed his secret!

"Anyway, whatever it was," Pru went on, "it was really brave of you, what you did, Gappy. Charging at Billy and Butch like that. You saved the day." She sighed. "I just hope we don't pay for it at school tomorrow. Billy probably feels pretty stupid right now."

"You're probably right," Gappy agreed as they reached Pru's corner. "We'll have to keep an eye out for Billy for a while, won't we? See ya, Pru."

Still shaking her head, Pru said goodbye and walked away down her street, turning after a few steps to wave back at Gappy.

Chapter Eight

Gappy is Grounded

As he continued on home, Gappy thought about Butch. *So, what just happened there?* he asked himself. *Could it be that mind-reading . . . er . . . telepathy stuff Mom and Dad were telling me about?*

He stooped to sniff some honeysuckle that was growing in Mrs. Pritchett's yard. *Mmm, they didn't say it worked on animals. I mean, when it first happened I wasn't even thinking of doing telepa-*

thy . . . didn't even know I could do it yet. After all, I only just found out about this vampire stuff yesterday. It really did seem like Butch heard me, though.

He took a deep breath and blew it out hard. *Wow! That was amazing. I wonder if I could do it again?*

He passed his neighbor's cat sitting on the wall cleaning herself. *Hello, Tabby,* he told her with his mind.

The cat ignored him and continued washing.

Hmm, Gappy thought. *My head doesn't feel as clear as it did at the old house when I was so angry at Billy. Maybe it was feeling angry that made my thoughts more powerful.*

He shifted his book bag to his other shoulder. *I can sort of understand now why a vampire's talents can be a big responsibility. I'm not sure how what I just did fits in with the Vampire Code of Conduct but, hey, I helped Timmy out, didn't I?*

As Gappy said this to himself, a warm, fuzzy feeling started spreading throughout his whole body. He felt so excited, it was difficult not to run down the street yelling and screaming at the top of his voice.

Then he calmed down a little when he thought about what Mom's reaction might be. He had a feeling she wouldn't be too happy at his news.

"Too soon, too soon," he muttered, imitating Mom. "Oh well, she'll just have to accept it. It wasn't *my* fault. It's not like I *tried* to do it. It just happened."

He reached his house and raced up the steps to the front door.

"Mom!" he yelled as he burst into the

house like a tornado, throwing his book bag on the floor and nearly knocking over Mom's favorite vase of artificial ferns. "Guess what *I* did!"

"What's that, dear?" Mom called from the living room.

"Just something totally awesome and amazing!" Gappy said excitedly, running into the living room and throwing himself down on the couch. "You know that bully, Billy Tompkins? Well, Pru and I caught him bullying Timmy Daylo at that empty house on our way home from school. He was threatening to smash Timmy's model of the White House that he and his dad had made. You should see it, Mom. It's really great. It took them ages to put together, and Mr. Dempsey even put it in the glass case at the front of the school where all the trophies are.

"Anyway, Billy was going to smash it. His dog Butch was there too, looking pretty scary. Like, growling and everything. Pru and I stopped, but we couldn't really do anything. Like, Billy's bigger than me and much bigger than Pru."

"So, *like,* what happened then?" Mom asked, smiling at his excitement.

"Well, I had to try and do something, so I ran up to the house, and I just happened to be looking at Butch and thinking he was a stupid dog, when he yelped like he heard me. That made me think of the mind-reading thing we were talking about last night, so I decided to try it on Butch. I beamed a thought at him to go home and . . . guess what, Mom?"

Mom straightened up from unwinding the

cord of the vacuum cleaner and stood dead still, a frown on her face. "What?" she said in a stern voice.

Uh oh, Gappy thought, but he had started his story so he decided to finish.

"Well, I couldn't believe it. Butch actually put his tail between his legs and started running home like I'd told him to. Billy was so surprised that by the time he chucked Timmy's model off the porch, I'd managed to get close enough to catch it. Billy ran off after Butch, really mad that I'd spoiled his little bit of bullying, and Timmy –"

Gappy trailed off at the worsening look on his mother's face. "What's the matter, Mom?"

His mother sat down on the edge of Gappy's chair and drilled him with her eyes. "This is just great, Gappy. Exactly the sort of thing I was afraid might happen, if we gave you too much information too soon. For goodness sake! You only just found out that you're a vampire, and the next day you're already playing around with skills like telepathy?"

"I knew you wouldn't be very happy at my news," Gappy said, "but I couldn't just walk on by and do nothing, could I?"

"I don't know, Gappy, but you've got to realize. These talents you're going to be developing as time goes on aren't toys for you to just play with whenever you want. It's like playing with fire. You're too young and you don't know how dangerous it can be. What's especially dangerous is the risk of regular humans finding out what you can do. We talked about this last night, but I'm going to tell you again. If regs found out, who knows what would happen? Not to mention getting us all into trouble with the Vampire Council. They'd probably have to do some major damage control, and . . . "

Vampire Council? Gappy thought. *What's that? Some kind of vampire government agency? Well, Mom sure won't be pleased if I tell her Pru just about hit the nail on the head. Anyway, I'm sure Pru doesn't really believe I actually beamed thoughts at Butch, so I guess I'll keep it to myself.*

"Okay, Mom," he broke in when his mother paused for breath. "I'm really sorry, but I don't think you have to worry. Billy and Pru and Timmy don't know anything. They might think it a bit strange the way Butch acted, but they just think he got spooked by something and ran off, that's all. No harm done."

"Well, we'll see," Mom said. "Just cross your fingers that your little *escapade* doesn't get noticed in some high-up places. My nerves are going to be all shot now, waiting to hear if we're going to be disciplined by the Council. You can't hide anything from those people. They always find out somehow."

Gappy didn't like the sound of that. "What will they do, Mom?"

But his mother was done talking. She got up quickly and yanked the vacuum cleaner toward her by its cord as if she were mad at that too. "Go to your room," she ordered, "and don't come down 'til your father gets home."

"But, Mom," Gappy wailed.

"But nothing, Gustavus," Mom told him sternly. "Up to your room!"

Muttering to himself, Gappy did as he was told and trudged up the stairs. He felt cross that instead of praising him for being a hero, Mom was mad at him.

And it's not even that big a deal, he thought. *What did I do? Just beam thoughts at a stupid dog. Not even people.*

He threw himself on his bed and opened his textbook. How was he supposed to concentrate on geography when all he could think about was what was going to happen when Dad came home? Mom was probably going to push for some kind of punishment too.

When Dad arrived, Gappy could hear his mother telling him about his so-called *escapade*. Judging by the way her voice was growing louder and louder, it sounded as if she were getting pretty upset all over again.

Gappy is Grounded

Muttering to himself, Gappy did as he was told and trudged up the stairs.

"Gappy, get down here," she eventually yelled up the stairs.

Gappy went down to the living room. Mom looked like she had been crying, but Dad did not look *too* mad, thank goodness.

"Gappy, Mom told me about what you did today," Dad began, "and I want you to know I agree with her totally. It's very dangerous to go playing around with your skills, willy-nilly, whenever you feel like it, especially when you're so new at this vampire business and don't know anything yet.

"It's also true that the Vampire Council may very well get involved." He put on a pompous voice as if he were quoting from a book. "Any act by a vampire that threatens to expose our people, or risks destroying our harmonious co-existence with regs, is taken

72

very seriously indeed. Yes, even when it's a mere nine-year-old, inexperienced vampire. After all, you could be putting the whole vampire race in danger."

Gappy tried to butt in, but Dad waved him to be quiet and listen.

"Now, from what I understand, it's likely no harm has been done this time because the regs didn't know what they were seeing. Is that correct?"

"Yes, Dad," Gappy mumbled, looking down at his shoes.

"All right, then. Let this be a lesson to you, and listen carefully." He put on his pompous voice again. "Do not use any vampire skills in the presence of regular humans, or in any situation where regular humans might see or suddenly come upon you doing any kind of vampire activity. Is that clear?"

"Yes, Dad," Gappy mumbled again. "But, Dad, seeing as I don't know what other skills I might be developing as time goes on, how can I guard against them?"

"You'll know," Dad said, "and I think I do now agree with Mom when she says she doesn't want to tell you too much too soon. We told you about telepathy, and look what happened."

He looked at Gappy's crestfallen face. "Don't worry. All your skills will show themselves gradually, and we'll handle them one at a time as they appear. Mom's right when she says you should have as normal a childhood as possible because there are going to be times ahead when it won't be so easy.

"Now, your mother and I have discussed

your punishment, and we've decided to ground you for a week."

"Aw, Dad!" Gappy protested. "A whole week? Don't I get any credit for helping Timmy get rid of a bully?"

"I'm sure that was very admirable," Mom put in, "but vampire safety comes first, and you have to learn that."

"Yeah, okay," Gappy pouted, "I get it." Shoot! Now he would have to make some excuse to Pru as to why he could not go to the movie they had planned to see that weekend. He could not very well tell her his parents had grounded him for being a hero, could he?

Dad looked at Mom. "So, dear, why don't we all have some dinner and try to forget about this for now, if we can?"

"What about the Vampire Council?" Mom

asked. "I'm going to be worrying myself sick, thinking about what they're going to say when they find out about this."

"Well, at this point we don't even know that they *will* find out," Dad reasoned, "and you can't be worrying yourself about something that might never happen. This incident concerned only a dog, so maybe the Council won't consider it important enough to bother about. We'll just have to wait and hope for the best."

"I hope you're right, Burt," Mom said, eyeing Gappy's sulky face.

"I really hope you're right."

The End

Acknowledgments

A huge thank you to Briony Allan, my daughter and friend, who is such a great sounding board for bouncing around story ideas, editing issues, and names of characters — sometimes late at night. Livinia thanks you too, Briony.

Many thanks also go to 10-year-old Will Kachidurian, who worked hard on the proof-reading and made very helpful editing suggestions.

And, finally, a big thank you to Edith Bakker, who first suggested the idea of Gappy when I was an 11-year-old student, struggling to think of ideas for a homework essay.

Visit Gappy at

www.gappy.tv

Breinigsville, PA USA
14 October 2009
225808BV00001B/2/P